T5-CUU-816

THE SWAMPEES

DOUBLE CROSS!

BY GILLIAN OSBAND
ILLUSTRATED BY BOBBIE SPARGO

PATTI THE APATOSAURUS

P.T. THE PTERANODON

ELLA THE ELASMOSAURUS

REX THE TYRANNOSAURUS

STIGGY THE STEGOSAURUS

MAX THE WOOLLY MAMMOTH

FRANKLIN WATTS
New York / London / Toronto / Sydney / 1982
Copyright © 1982 by Manor Lodge Productions, Ltd. All rights reserved. Printed in Belgium.

WELCOME TO SWAMP VALLEY...

Far away is a valley where life has remained unchanged for fifty million years.

This is Swamp Valley, home of the Swampees.

"That's us!"

Meet Max, the leader of the Swampees.

Patti is always ready to help.

Stiggy is the inventor and mission controller.

P.T. is ready for takeoff.

And there's never been an Elasmosaurus like Ella.

Last, but not least, is Rex.

Friends everywhere are Swampee Scouts.

This is Dr. Croc—the Swampees' enemy.

He lives in Crocodile Swamp.

It was a cold and windy day in Swamp Valley.

Rex was making pancakes with different mixtures that Stiggy had invented.

Patti was painting a picture of Rex.

Ella had a new fitness book and was trying out some of the exercises.

Max was reading the Swampee Diary.

Max suddenly jumped up.

"I've got an idea. Let's have a festival. Swampee Scouts from all over the world can come. And we will have a special Great Treasures of the World exhibition."

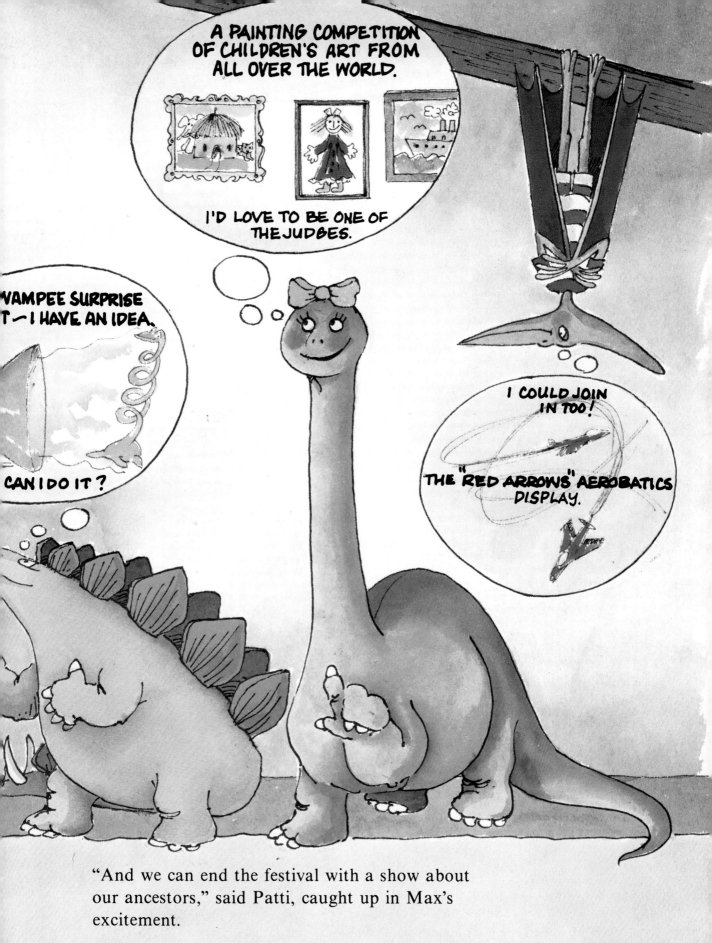

"And we can end the festival with a show about our ancestors," said Patti, caught up in Max's excitement.

"I will make it extra spectacular," said Stiggy, "with a Top Secret surprise!"

Max decided the festival would take place in Edinburgh Castle, in Scotland.

For the next few weeks, the Swampees were very busy.

Patti planned the activities and the show.

Rex set up the campsite.

Ella and P.T. raced around getting the decorations, seats, and microphones ready.

Max arranged the Great Treasures of the World exhibition. The Swampee Scouts were bringing a special treasure from each of their countries.

And Stiggy was inventing something for the Swampee Spectacular.

Meanwhile, in Croc Grotto, Dr. Croc had decided to give the festival his own surprise.

He wanted the Great Treasures of the World collection for his own. He already had a special cave to put it in. All he had to do now was get it!

"I want the Swampees watched at all times," he roared at his henchmen.

I WILL CALL IT THE "DR CROC COLLECTIO

Stiggy came racing out of the cave. "I've done it!" he called to the others. "I've invented a Lasergram!"

He fitted some special plates into the machine he was carrying. There, right before them, was a giant picture of Rex himself!

"That's incredible!" said Patti. "And there isn't even a screen."

"We will put on our show at midnight, on the top of the hill outside the city," said Max.

"And we will all be giant size!" said Max.

YOU NEED A SPECIAL LASER, A BEAM-SPLITTER, SPECIAL LENSES... ....

Dr. Croc's eyes gleamed when he heard about Stiggy's Lasergram. "I can steal the Great Treasures of the World and make a fool of the Swampees at the same time. Arrange a peace meeting with them at once!"

"Well! What do you know!" exclaimed Max. "Dr. Croc wants a peace meeting with us about the festival. We must all go to the meeting place."

"We'll call a special truce," said Dr. Croc, "provided we are allowed to put on our own show."

"Agreed," said Max. "Trust has to start somewhere. We will fit you into the show."

"The Highland Flingers will put on a show," laughed Dr. Croc. "We will *borrow* Stiggy's Lasergram. Everyone will think it is us, but we will be stealing the treasure!"

Everything was ready just in time for the start of the festival.

The Swampees collected all the Swampee Scouts and the special treasures and brought them to Edinburgh.

Property Of
COLFAX-MINGO COMMUNITY SCHOOL
COLFAX, IOWA

The festival camp was a flurry of activity. There were last minute rehearsals, and costumes that needed mending.

Ella and P.T. had decided to keep an eye on Dr. Croc, but they were so busy they didn't see him sneak into Stiggy's tent.

The Great Treasures of the World exhibition was a big success.

"With everyone watching us *perform* our Scottish dances, we can load everything into the Croc-copter with no problem," Dr. Croc thought happily.

All too quickly the last day of the festival arrived.

Everyone had seen wonderful dancing, music, and singing from each Swampee group.

Dr. Croc and his Highland Flingers were performing at the end of the day.

Suddenly something very strange began to happen. Dr. Croc and his henchmen began to fade before their eyes!

"We've been tricked. They must have used Stiggy's **Lasergram**. Dr. Croc's not here at all," cried Max. "He's after the Great Treasures! P.T., go and look for him, but don't let him see you."

At the exhibition hall, Dr. Croc and his henchmen were busy.

"Form a line and get the Croc-copter loaded quickly!" said Dr. Croc.

P.T. watched from above. He was waiting for Dr. Croc to go into the hall for a final pick of the treasure.

P.T. swooped down and untied the loading baskets.

Max knew that they had to act quickly to stop Dr. Croc. They had all grabbed something that made a noise.

"Surround the Croc-copter, but you must not be seen. Don't make a sound until you get the signal," Max said quietly.

"I've got an extra surprise for Dr. Croc," said Stiggy.

As Dr. Croc climbed into the Croc-copter, Max gave the signal.